The Adventures of
Naya and Gumbo
Case of the Worries

Priya K. Tahim

This is a work of fiction. All of the characters, names, incidents, organizations, and dialogue in this novel are either the products of the author's imagination or are used fictitiously.

Archway Publishing books may be ordered through booksellers or by contacting:

Archway Publishing
1663 Liberty Drive
Bloomington, IN 47403
www.archwaypublishing.com
844-669-3957

ISBN: 978-1-6657-0166-2 (sc)
ISBN: 978-1-6657-0167-9 (hc)
ISBN: 978-1-6657-0168-6 (e)

Print information available on the last page.

Archway Publishing rev. date: 3/18/2021

The characters in this book are inspired by my adorable niece, Anaya and her best pal, Gumbo. Anaya, you are a true gift and I'm so lucky to play the role of "Masi mama" in your life.

To my grandparents: Papa-ji, Bibi, Nana-ji and Nani, thank you for being the most inspiring humans in my life. You are the reason we learned the meaning of hard work and family.

To my parents, whom I would never have had the courage to share my writings without. Thank you for being my biggest critic and cheerleaders.

To my sisters, whom ironically are my best friends...Thank you for always supporting me with whatever adventure I choose to go on. Nauraj Jij, from day one you've always shown me brotherly love and I'm so glad you brought Gumbo (the real MVP) into our lives.

Bubby, my wonderfully talented husband. Thank you for always pushing me to be better, do better, and to put myself out there.

Lastly, this book is dedicated to all those children (and adults) who ever felt like they didn't have a voice. Don't ever let someone take your voice away.

"I'm a very strong believer in listening
and learning from others."
—Ruth Bader Ginsburg

—Priya Tahim

"Gumbo, are you ready?" screamed Naya, as she grabbed her handy dandy backpack.

"Ready…ready for what?" Gumbo questioned, as he wagged his tail.

"Ready for our BIG day! Our day full of fun, exploring, learning, and the best part…ADVENTURES!" Naya leaped up and down, full of excitement, as she ran towards her pal to give him a hug.

Gumbo's tummy began to fill with butterflies, as his tail began to drop.

Before Naya could wrap her tiny arms around her furry sidekick, Gumbo cried out, "WOAHHH! Hold your tails, I'm not ready for fun. I'm not ready for excitement, and most importantly, I'm not ready for adventures. My backpack is not packed. My tail is not wagging, and most of all, I have butterflies in my tummy!"

As Naya looked around and explored the room, she noticed Gumbo's backpack unpacked, his tail not wagging, and his body a tad bit shy.

"Hmm…" Naya thought to herself. "How can I help Gumbo get ready? How can I help him shake his worries away?"

Naya thought back to when she felt worried. She remembered a plan her parents helped her come up with to shake her worries away. Naya began to smile.

"I KNOW!" Naya shouted with glee, "Let's make a plan!"

"A plan…what do you mean", whispered Gumbo.

"A plan to help you feel safe! All we need is to think with our brains, feel with our hearts, and shout the magic words: I think I can, I know I can, shake the worries away. In my heart, I know what's best, now let's put this plan to the test!"

"Come on Gumbo, say it with me: I think I can, I know I can, shake the worries away. In my heart, I know what's best, now let's put this plan to the test!"

Naya and Gumbo put their brains together, to come up with a plan.

Naya excitedly said, "First thing's first, we have to shout out something special about ourselves. You first Gumbo, what is special about you?"

Gumbo thought long and hard about what to say, before replying "I don't feel so special, and I don't know what to say."

Naya looked at Gumbo and grabbed his paw. As she held on to his furry paw, she said, "You are special, you're special to me. Being your pal, fills me with glee."

Gumbo looked up at Naya, and saw her great, big, beautiful smile. His tail began to raise, and his heart began to beat faster and faster. Gumbo closed his eyes, and slowly started to chant, "I think I can, I know I can, shake the worries away. In my heart, I know what's best, now let's put this plan to the test!"

"Next, we jump around, to let the worry bug out." Naya screamed, as she put music on.

"Dance with me Gumbo!"

Naya and Gumbo began to dance to their favorite song. Before Gumbo knew it, his tail was wagging, and his worries were gone. As they danced, they both sang, "I think I can, I know I can, shake the worries away. In my heart, I know what's best, now let's put this plan to the test!"

Naya smiled and said, "Now, all you have to do is remember, you are special, you are brave, and now the worry bug is gone. If it comes back, you know what to do."

Gumbo smiled, as he began to shout, "I think I can, I know I can, shake the worries away. In my heart, I know what's best, now let's put this plan to the test!" Gumbo gathered his things and packed his backpack.

Naya and Gumbo danced their worries away and went on to enjoy their day full of adventure.

_____'s Worry plan

(insert your name here)

Something special about me is: _____

_____.

My "happy song" is: _____.

When I am feeling worried I can talk to _____,

_____ and _____.

Things that make me feel better: _____

_____ and _____.

"I think I can, I Know I can, shake the worries away. In my heart, I Know what's best, now let's put this plan to the test!"

Printed in the United States
by Baker & Taylor Publisher Services